To my two darlings, Álvaro and Pablo.

Paula Merlán

To my family.

Gómez

The Finger and the Nose
Somos8 Series

© Text: Paula Merlán, 2018
© Illustrations: Gómez, 2018
© Edition: NubeOcho, 2019
www.nubeocho.com · hello@nubeocho.com

Original title: *El dedo en la nariz*
English translation: Ben Dawlatly
Text editing: Rebecca Packard, Eva Burke
and Céline Siret

Distributed in the United States by
Consortium Book Sales & Distribution

First edition: 2019
ISBN: 978-84-17123-78-9

Printed in Portugal.

VALUES,
FUN &
DIVERSITY

THE FINGER AND THE NOSE

PAULA MERLÁN

ILLUSTRATED BY GÓMEZ

nubeOCHO

YOUR NOSE IS GOING TO END UP HUGE!

Her parents would tell her this over and over.
The thing was... Sophie had a bad habit.

She would fly Tim, the index finger of her left hand, right up her nose.

Sophie did it all the time...

while she was
feeding Milo,

while she was coloring her
animal drawings...

and as she was chewing
mint-flavored gum.

Inside Sophie's nose there wasn't much
light, but it was nice and warm.
Little by little, Tim turned that space into
his home.

At the entrance of the nose, Tim hung a giant sign.

He also set up a living room with a comfortable armchair so he could watch TV. When he got bored, he'd go to the kitchen and enjoy the wonderful tasting menu.

Tim's best friend, Bob the finger, would pop over from time to time, and he would rustle up some delicious treats for him.

Slimy chocolate cake
was his favorite.

After dinner, Tim liked to sit back in his chair and read one of the books from his library. Some of his favorite titles were *The Big Bad Finger* and *Three Little Digits*.

TOM THUMB

THE BIG BAD FINGER

3 LITTLE DIGITS

1, 2, 3

3RD EDITION

One day Sophie was looking in the mirror and saw that her nose had become gigantic.

OooooHHHHH !

"My nose looks like a turnip!"
"Who's shouting and screaming?"
"Mom! My nose is as big as a giant's nose."
"We told you, Sophie, but you never listened…"

"What can I do?"

"Dunk it in cold water?"

"Ask it to shrink?"

"Hide it with a baseball cap?"

"Oh Sophie, you can figure it out for yourself.
Take a good look and think about what you need to do."

Sophie started to think through everything she did on a typical day. Soon she realized that Tim would take a trip into her nose anytime he could.

"Tim, do you know why my nose
has grown?" Sophie asked.

"Well, you've been bringing me to your nose for years."

"Seriously?" Sophie asked, puzzled.

"I've made it my home. Inside, I've got a living room, a kitchen, a library…" Tim replied.

"How could you do this to me?" Sophie asked.

"And if you give me enough time, I'll be able to build a park with slides, swings and flower beds," Tim added.

"No, please! If you keep on building things up there,
my nose will hit the floor!"

Tim didn't know what to do. He wanted to help Sophie, but how could he do it without losing his lovely home?

"You don't want to kick me out, do you? Who's going to keep me cozy and warm?

"Who will cook slimy chocolate cake for me?

"And most importantly, how will I read my favorite books?"

"I'll make all of that happen," Sophie reassured him.

"I guess that's fine," Tim responded. "It's up to your hand."

Sophie pondered the situation… Her finger was right.
She was the one responsible for making her nose grow
so big! Her parents had told her loads of times.

Ever since then, Sophie has been careful about picking her nose. And Tim now has a jacket so he doesn't get cold. He's cozy and warm!

Each time Sophie makes
a cake at home, she lets
him try it first.

When she reads her favorite books,
she uses her finger to track the words so
Tim feels like he's the star of the story.

Sophie and Tim are happy,
and, little by little, her nose is
going back to its normal size.

However, there's someone at home who's still got a lot to learn…

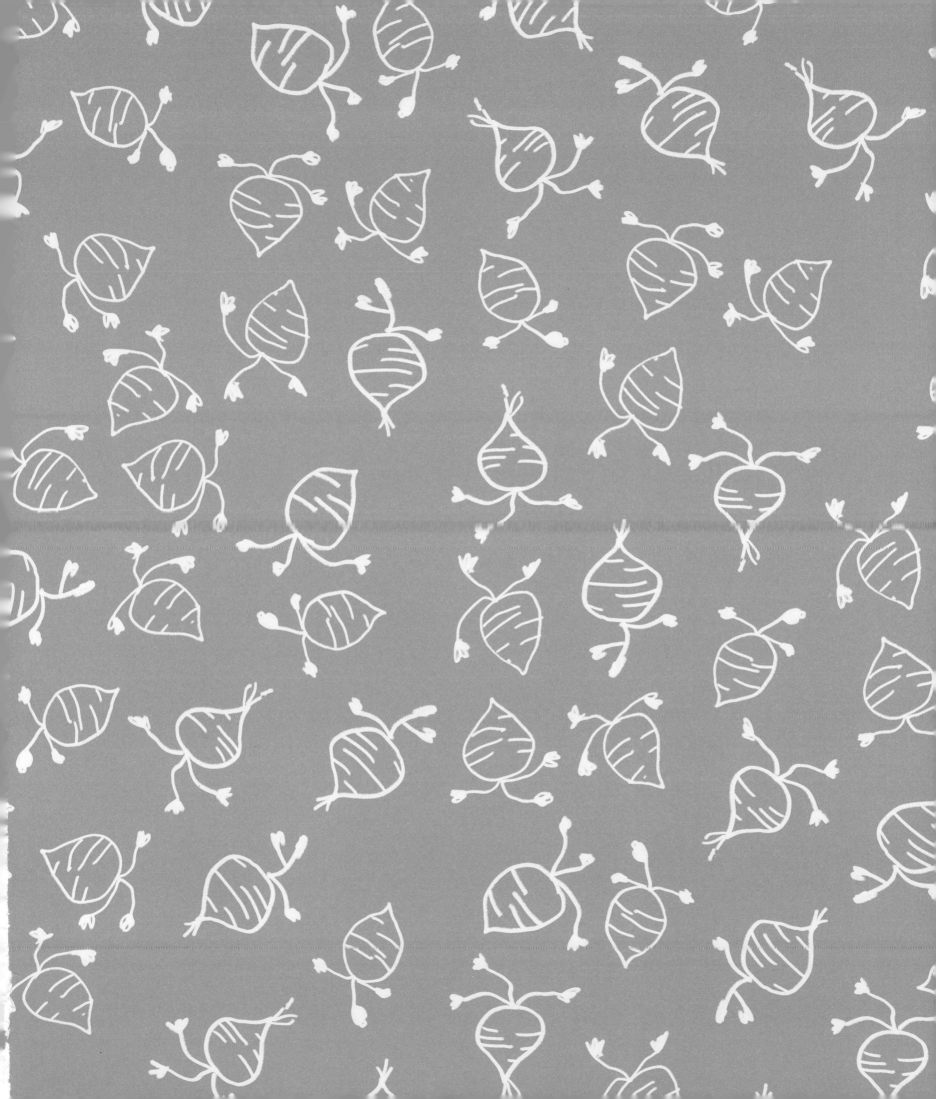

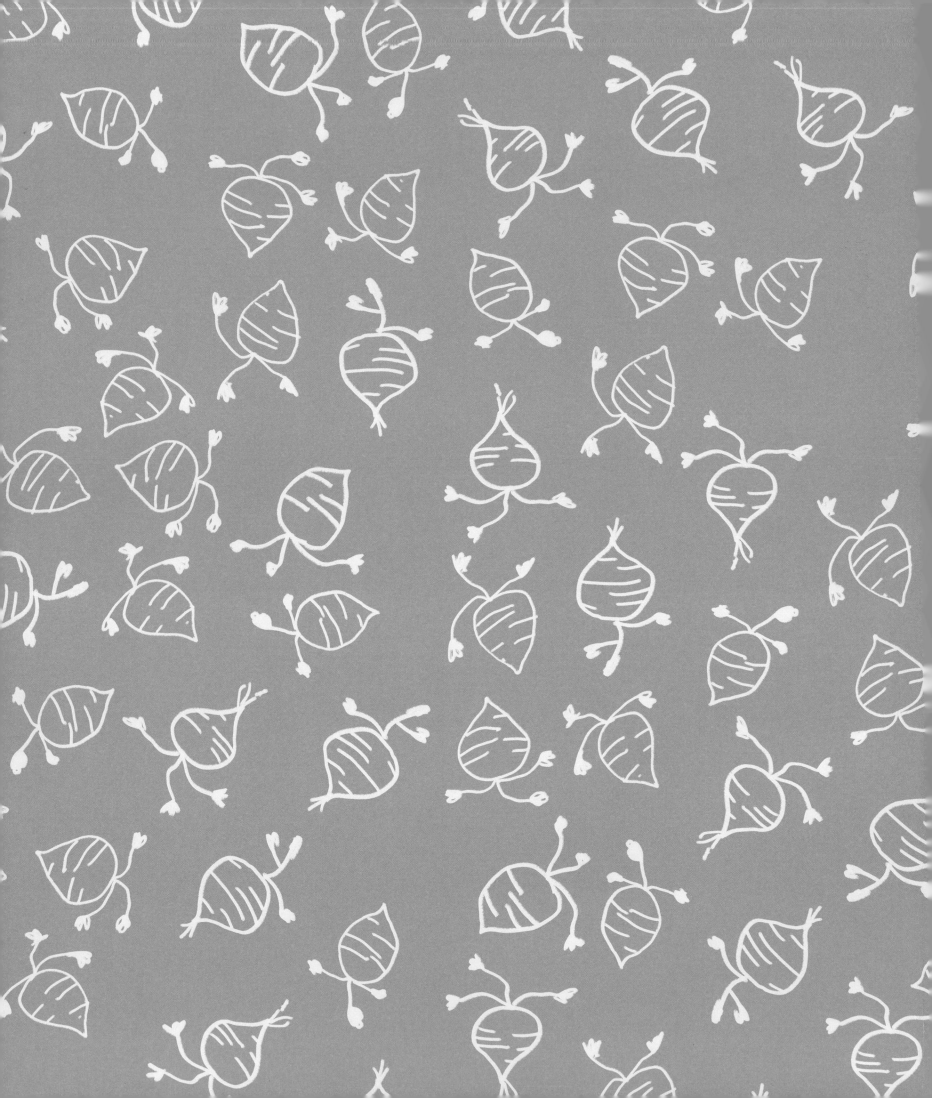